HOPSCOTCH FAIRY TALES

Cinderella

by Anne Cassidy and Jan McCafferty

W
FRANKLIN WATTS
LONDON • SYDNEY

Once upon a time there was
a girl called Cinderella.
She was not happy.

5

Cinderella had two stepsisters.
One was tall and one was small.
They made Cinderella work all
day long.

The stepsisters made Cinderella
wear horrible clothes.

And they made her sleep
by the fireplace.

One day a letter arrived.

"It's from the prince!" said the tall stepsister. "There's a ball at the palace!" said the small stepsister.

Everyone was excited – even
Cinderella. The stepsisters told her:
"But *you* can't come!"

After the stepsisters left for
the ball, Cinderella sat
by the fireplace.

"It's not fair," she said.

"I'd love to go to the ball!"

Suddenly there was a big flash.
It was a fairy with a wand!

"I'm your fairy godmother," she said.
"Now you can go to the ball!"

The fairy godmother waved her
wand. In another flash, Cinderella
had a new dress and sparkling
glass slippers.

15

Then the fairy godmother
saw a pumpkin ...

four black mice ...

and a rat.

She waved her wand and, in a
flash, there were four black horses
and a handsome coach driver.
"Here is your coach," she said.

"Now I really can go to the ball!"
said Cinderella.

"Be back before the clock strikes
twelve!" said the fairy godmother.

"Bye bye!" Cinderella said.

"Don't forget to be back by

twelve!" the fairy godmother

shouted.

When Cinderella arrived at the
ball, everyone looked at her.
"Who is she?" they wondered.

The stepsisters stared, and the
prince couldn't take his eyes off her.

"Will you dance with me?"
the prince asked Cinderella.

The prince and Cinderella
danced ...

and danced …

and danced all night.

23

Suddenly Cinderella heard the clock strike twelve. She ran out of the palace. The prince ran after her, but Cinderella was gone.

"Look! She has left a glass slipper behind!" the prince cried. "Whoever can fit into the slipper will be my princess," he promised.

The prince searched every house in the land. Finally, he arrived at Cinderella's house.

First, the tall sister tried the slipper on. But it was much too small.

Then the small stepsister tried it on. But it was much too big.

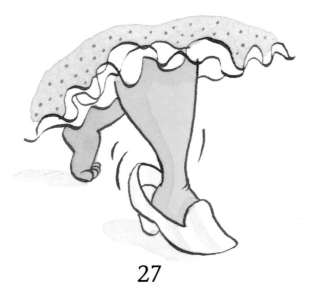

"Now this girl must try it on!"
the prince said.

"But that's just Cinderella!"
laughed the stepsisters.

Cinderella sat down. She tried the glass slipper on. It fitted perfectly.

"Will you be my princess?" asked the prince. Cinderella agreed and they lived happily ever after.

31

Hopscotch has been specially designed to fit the requirements of the National Literacy Strategy. It offers real books by top authors and illustrators for children developing their reading skills. There are 43 Hopscotch stories to choose from:

* hardback